HOW SNOWSHOE HARE RESCUED THE SUN

A Tale from the Arctic

retold by Emery Bernhard

illustrated by Durga Bernhard

HOLIDAY HOUSE · NEW YORK

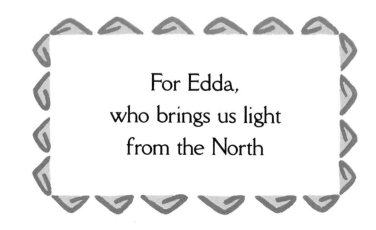

For Edda,
who brings us light
from the North

Library of Congress Cataloging-in-Publication Data
Bernhard, Emery.
How Snowshoe Hare rescued the sun : a tale from the Arctic / retold by
Emery Bernhard ; illustrated by Durga Bernhard. — 1st ed.
p.   cm.
Summary: When the demons who live under the earth steal the sun
leaving the tundra in darkness, the animals send Bear, Wolf, and
finally Snowshoe Hare to bring it back.
ISBN 0-8234-1043-9
1. Yuit Eskimos — Legends.   [1. Eskimos — Russia — Legends.]
I. Bernhard, Durga, ill.   II. Title.
E99.E7B44   1993   92-47124   CIP   AC
398.2′089971 — dc20
[E]

Grateful acknowledgment is made to Interlink Publishing Group, Inc. for
"How the Sun Was Rescued" from *The Sun Maiden and the Crescent
Moon: Siberian Folk Tales*. Copyright © 1989 by James Riordan. Published
by Interlink Books, an imprint of Interlink Publishing Group, Inc.

About This Book

How Snowshoe Hare Rescued the Sun is adapted from "How the Sun Was Rescued" in James Riordan's fine collection of Siberian folktales, *The Sun Maiden and the Crescent Moon*. Riordan's source was a storyteller among the seacoast dwellers at the north-eastern tip of Siberia. These Siberian natives are also called the Yuit. For centuries, they crossed back and forth from Siberia to North America in their tough walrus-skin boats. The Yuit share language, culture, and stories with their Inuit relatives across the Bering Strait in Alaska.

Throughout the Far North, there are tales of a primordial darkness that existed until Raven or Hare restored light to the world. Other animals move freely in and out of Arctic tales . . . sometimes as tricksters, sometimes as heroes. To people who have hunted for thousands of years, animals easily embody both the wisdom and folly of humans. And on such a desolate landscape, the distinctive character of each animal stands out.

Snowshoe Hare, quiet and brave, is my favorite.

—E.B.

The pictures in this book were painted in gouache on top of transparent layered "veils" of permanent acrylic color. Some final touches were added in colored pencil. The characters were inspired by ritual masks and carved objects of native peoples of Alaska and Siberia and by contemporary Inuit stonecut prints. The color scheme of the book—painted in the dead of winter in the Catskills—was inspired by the view from my studio window of the play of changing light on distant mountains and snowfields.

—D.B.

In a time long past, the demons who live under the earth decided to steal the Sun. It was autumn, after the first ice storm had warned of the great cold to come. The greedy demons wanted the Sun for themselves and did not care if everyone else froze.

With night falling and the last snow geese flying south, the demons made a ladder to the sky. The biggest demon grabbed a harpoon and climbed up on the backs of his brothers. He hurled his harpoon deep into the heart of the setting Sun. Then all the demons began to pull hard on the long harpoon line.

The next morning, the Sun did not come up. The animals of the tundra awoke and peered into the darkness. Expecting daylight, they blinked and stumbled into each other. Expecting the Sun's warmth, they shivered in the chill wind and huddled close to the mossy earth.

In those days there was no Moon or Stars, and only the shimmering Northern Lights brightened the gloom.

The animals of the land and beasts of the sea and birds of the air gathered for a great council. Old Snowy Owl spoke first.

"Friends, how much longer can we live in this darkness that never ends? Without the Sun, spring will never come. I, who rest during the day, do not know when to go to sleep. I, who fly at night, saw demons dragging the Sun away to their cavern under the mountains. Who will rescue the Sun?"

Raven began croaking loudly and hopping from rock to rock.

"I, whom all know to be wise, advise that we send the strongest among us—the Bear."

"The Bear! The Bear!" everyone cried.

"Who, who?" asked old Snowy Owl, who was almost deaf.

"We're sending Bear!" bellowed Walrus.

"Oh no," screeched Owl. "As soon as Bear gets hungry, he'll forget about rescuing the Sun."

"I will not," growled Bear, standing tall. "I will return with the Sun."

Bear charged out over the tundra, but once he was out of sight he began to shamble and sniff and swing his head this way and that. He nosed into a shrubby bog and slowly scraped the snow away from some berry bushes.

It took a long time for Bear to find enough berries to fill his belly.

It did not take so long for the other animals to realize that Bear had forgotten about the Sun.

Raven spoke again. "Let's send Wolf. He's faster than Bear, and almost as strong."

"The Wolf! The Wolf!" cried the animals.

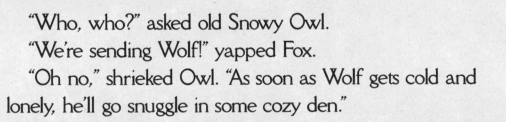

"Who, who?" asked old Snowy Owl.

"We're sending Wolf!" yapped Fox.

"Oh no," shrieked Owl. "As soon as Wolf gets cold and lonely, he'll go snuggle in some cozy den."

Wolf yawned. "I'm not afraid of the cold or the demons."

Wolf stretched and trotted off. A fierce north wind stung
his muzzle and whipped his fur, seeping cold into his bones.
When he heard the lonesome call of a faraway wolf, he

stopped, raised his nose to the dark sky, and let out a long, loud howl of his own. Soon Wolf found the den. He curled up in the snug darkness with the other wolves and fell asleep.

Weeks passed. There was no sign of Wolf. Once again the animals met in the darkness. Just as Raven was about to speak, tiny Lemming ran squeaking into the council circle.

"We should send Snowshoe Hare. He's the fastest runner."

"The Hare? The Hare?" everyone asked.

"Who, who?" demanded old Snowy Owl.

"Snowshoe Hare!" barked Seal.

The animals of the land and beasts of the sea and birds of the air all turned to old Snowy Owl.

"Hmmmmmm," said Owl, blinking. "Snowshoe Hare is the fastest runner in the snow. He can see well at night. And he's not selfish. He just might rescue the Sun!"

Snowshoe Hare twitched his
nose and bounded off on
his wide paws, hopping and
skipping over the snowy
plains toward the mountains.
For many days he traveled.
He passed a rare stretch of
grass but did not stop to eat.
A sudden snow squall nearly
blinded him, but he did not
seek shelter in the rough
tunnels of the old stone hills.

At last, Snowshoe Hare saw
bright rays of light beaming
from under the earth
through a crevice in the
mountain rock. He padded
over to the crack and
peered in.

A roaring, spinning ball of fire blazed away in a stone cauldron. Flames spilled out and lit up a vast cavern filled with bones. In the farthest corner of the cavern—snoring like distant thunder—slept the demons who live under the earth.

Snowshoe Hare slipped through the crack. Hopping quietly over to the cauldron, he pushed hard with his strong hind legs and knocked it over. The ball of fire rolled free, and in a flash Hare kicked it through the crack and leaped out of the cavern.

The demons woke screaming and rushed after Snowshoe
Hare, pushing and fighting each other to squeeze through the
crack. Hare kicked the ball of fire across the frozen earth.
Then he turned and ran after it as fast as he could.

But as fast as he was, the furious demons were even faster. Hare knew they would soon catch him and tear him limb from limb.

Just as the demons were about to grab him, Snowshoe Hare kicked the ball of fire up into the sky. He kicked it so hard that it broke into flaming pieces. The biggest piece flew high into the heavens and became the Sun. A large chunk soared up to become the Moon. And many small embers zoomed out to become all the Stars in the Milky Way.

The new Sun flew higher and burned brighter than the old Sun, and the greedy demons were instantly blinded by its light. They scampered back to their cavern under the earth and have never again been seen above the ground.

Spring came to the tundra in one day. The animals of the land and beasts of the sea and birds of the air all praised the brave Snowshoe Hare who had rescued the Sun.

And old Snowy Owl again had the sunrise to tell him when it was time to go to sleep in his nest.